A Frog in the Bog

To my wonderful agent, Steve, who helped me make it in the frog-eat-bug world of writing
– K. W.

For Lana and Chris. In memory of your childhood
– J. R.

◙ ◙ ◉ ◙ ◙

SIMON &
SCHUSTER

First published in Great Britain in 2003 by Simon & Schuster UK Ltd
Africa House, 64-78 Kingsway, London WC2B 6AH

First published in 2003 by McElderry Books, an imprint of Simon & Schuster
Children's Publishing Division, New York.

Text copyright © 2003 by Karma Wilson
Illustrations copyright © 2003 by Joan Rankin

A CIP catalogue record for this book is available from the British Library upon request

Book design by Kristin Smith
The text for this book was set in Gorilla.
The illustrations are rendered in watercolour.

ISBN 0 689 83730 5

Manufactured in China

1 3 5 7 9 10 8 6 4 2

karma wilson

joan rankin

A Frog
in the Bog

Simon & Schuster
LONDON

There's a frog on the log in the middle of the bog.

A small, green frog
on a half-sunk log
in the middle of the bog.

He flicks ONE tick
as it creeps up a stick.

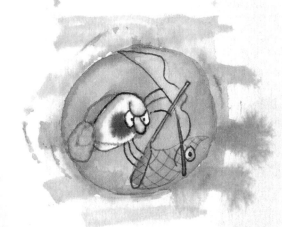

ONE tick in the belly of a small, green frog
on a half-sunk log
in the middle of the bog.

And the frog grows
a little bit
bigger...

He sees TWO fleas
as they leap through the reeds.

ONE tick, TWO fleas
in the belly of the frog
on a half-sunk log
in the middle of the bog.

And the frog grows
a little bit
bigger...

flyrodrome

He spies THREE flies
as they buzz through the skies.

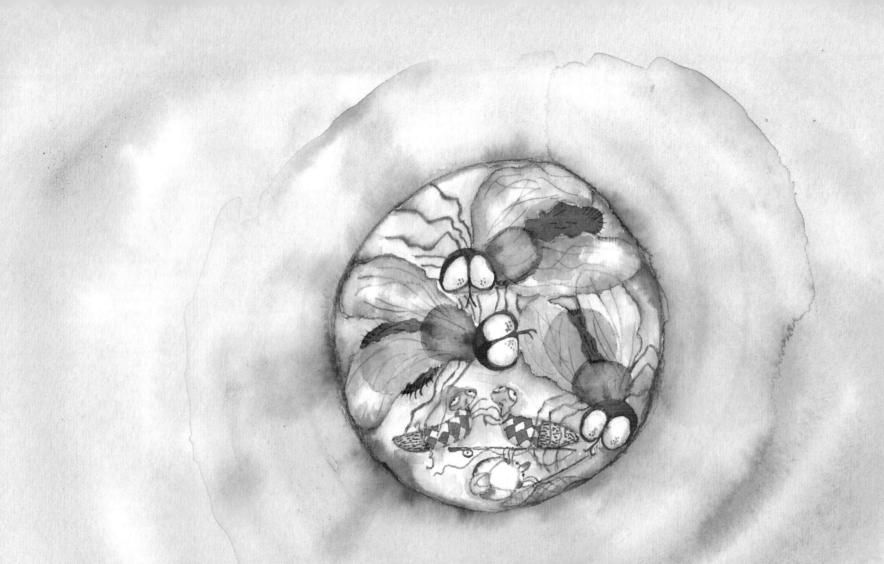

ONE tick, TWO fleas, THREE flies (Oh, my!)
in the belly of the frog
on a half-sunk log
in the middle of the bog.

And the frog grows
a little bit
bigger...

He glugs FOUR slugs
as they slink through the sludge.

ONE tick, **TWO** fleas, **THREE** flies (Oh, my!),
FOUR slugs (Ew, ugh!) in the belly of the frog
on a half-sunk log
in the middle of the bog.

And the frog grows
a little bit
bigger...

He inhales FIVE snails
from their heads to their tails!

ONE tick, TWO fleas, THREE flies (Oh, my!),
FOUR slugs (Ew, ugh!), and FIVE slimy snails
in the belly of the frog
on a half-sunk log
in the middle of the bog.

What a hog, that frog!

And the frog grows
a little bit
bigger!!!

Then...

that log with the frog
in the middle of the bog
starts to rise...

and the frog sees eyes!

And the frog sees claws
and a big set of jaws,
and a mouth like a crater!
And the frog screams,

With his mouth open wide,
all the bugs inside
start to crawl and fly
and to slither and slide.

Out come FIVE snails
from their heads to their tails,

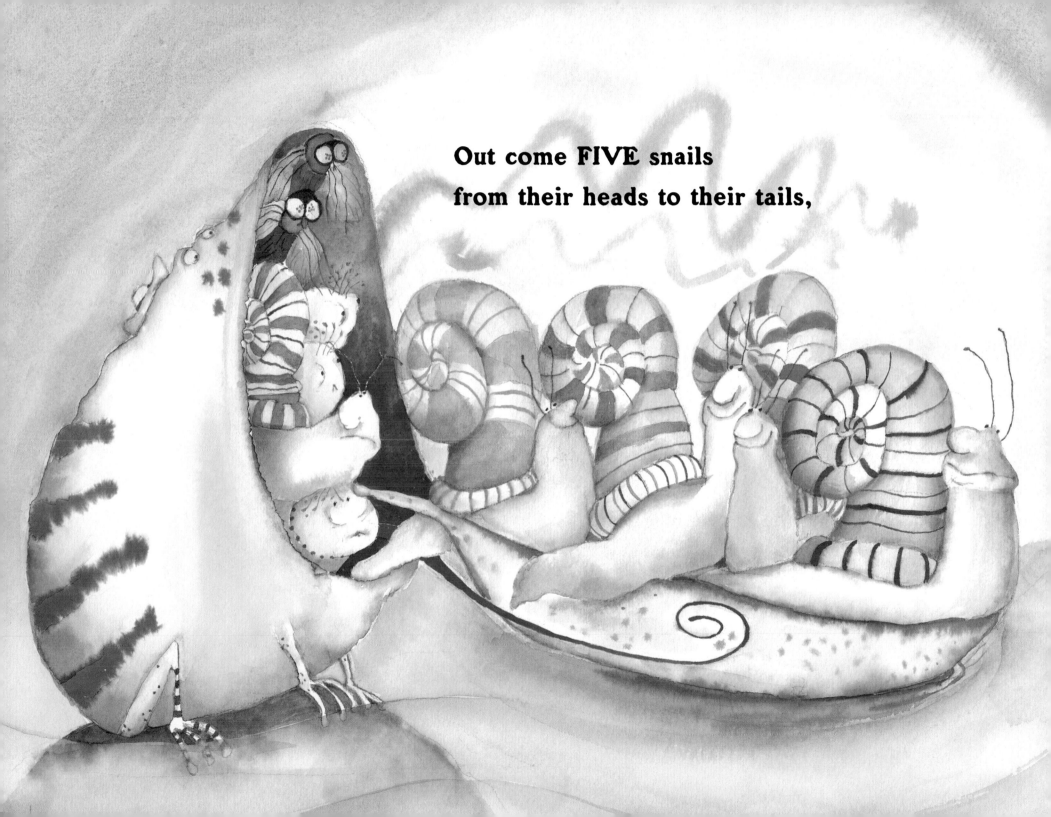

FOUR slugs (Ew, ugh!),

TWO fleas (Dear me!),

and ONE tiny tick.

ICK!

And right in the middle of his holler,

that frog grows
a whole lot

smaller...

"See ya later," says the alligator
as he romps through the swamp,
cuz the itty-bitty frog
isn't big enough to chomp.

Now...

Beetle Boats for Hire

the bugs in the bog
keep away from the frog,

and the frog NEVER sits on a half-sunk log!